THOMAS ALVA EDISON
Great Inventor

THOMAS ALVA EDISON

Great Inventor

A FIRST BIOGRAPHY

by DAVID A. ADLER

illustrated by Lyle Miller

Holiday House/New York

IMPORTANT DATES

1847   Born February 11 in Milan, Ohio.

1854   The Edison family moved to Port Huron, Michigan.

1863   Began work as a telegraph operator.

1869   Became a full-time inventor.

1871   Married Mary Stilwell.

1876   Opened laboratory in Menlo Park, New Jersey.

1877   Invented the phonograph.

1879   Invented the electric light bulb.

1884   Wife Mary died.

1886   Married Mina Miller.

1887   Moved his laboratory to West Orange, New Jersey.

1914   Fire destroyed his laboratory.

1931   Died on October 18 in West Orange, New Jersey.

CONTENTS

1. "Why don't you know?"

THOMAS ALVA EDISON was born on February 11, 1847, in Milan, Ohio. His father, Samuel, was tall and strong. He owned a mill which made wooden shingles. Using lumber from his mill and bricks, he built a seven-room house for his family.

Thomas's mother, Nancy, was a former teacher and the daughter of a minister. Thomas was their seventh child. He was curious and tried to learn as much as he could. Many years later he said, "We don't know one-millionth of one percent about anything."

Thomas was always asking questions. He asked so many questions that some people, including his own father, thought he was dull. Many times the people Thomas asked couldn't answer his questions. When they said, "I don't know," Thomas asked, "Why don't you know?"

Milan, Ohio was a busy town. It was built along the Huron River with a canal connecting it to Lake Erie. As a small boy, Thomas watched families in covered wagons pass through Milan on their way to find gold in California. He watched as loaded wagons emptied grain into warehouses. Later, the grain was loaded onto boats that were pulled by horses through the canal.

Thomas also watched the owner of the local flour mill, Sam Winchester, experiment with hydrogen. One time the hydrogen caught fire and one of his mills was destroyed. Later, Sam Winchester built a hydrogen-filled passenger balloon. He sat in the basket and released the ropes. The balloon carried him over Lake Erie and he disappeared.

Young Thomas had experiments of his own. He had seen a goose sit on some eggs and then watched as little goslings hatched. He wondered what would happen if he sat on some eggs, too. So Thomas made a nest and filled it with goose and chicken eggs. He sat on them, but nothing hatched.

When Thomas was six years old, he experimented with fire in his father's barn. The barn burned to the ground. Sam Edison had punished Thomas for his mischief before, but this time he was especially angry. He was determined to teach young Thomas a lesson. He gave his son a beating in the center of the town's square, where anyone who wanted to could watch.

A year before, when Thomas was five, he was involved in an even greater tragedy. He and a friend were swimming in a small creek, and the other boy disappeared in the water. Young Thomas waited until dark, but he never saw the boy again.

Thomas went home and didn't tell anyone what had happened. He ate dinner and went to sleep, but that night he was awakened. The townspeople had been searching for the boy and discovered that Thomas was with him earlier in the day. Thomas told them where they had been swimming. They soon found the boy's body. He had drowned in the creek.

2. Strange Odors, Smoke . . .

IN 1853, when Thomas was six years old, a railroad line was built that passed about ten miles to the north of Milan. Shipping by train cost less and was faster than shipping by boat through the Milan canal. Wagons loaded with grain no longer came to fill the warehouses and fewer ships passed through the canal. There was less business for everyone, including Samuel Edison. In the spring of 1854, the Edisons moved about one hundred miles west, to Port Huron, Michigan.

At about the time the Edisons moved, Thomas came down with scarlet fever. He was sick for quite a while and didn't begin school until the following year, when he was eight and a half years old. The school had one room and Reverend G. B. Engle and his wife were the teachers.

They taught their students to memorize facts and repeat them. But Thomas asked questions. He wanted to understand what he was learning. The Engles had no patience for him.

Thomas was restless. Sitting still for so long was difficult for him. Reverend Engle wore a long black frock coat and he carried a stick which he often used on restless, curious Thomas Edison.

Thomas was one of Reverend Engle's worst students. He once told a visitor that the boy was addled, confused. Thomas ran out of school and home to his mother. He told her what Reverend Engle had said.

Nancy Edison told the teacher that her son was not addled. She suggested that maybe the Engles just didn't know how to teach a bright boy like Thomas. She took him out of school and taught him herself. Thomas discovered that his mother was his "enthusiastic champion." He wrote later that he decided "right then that I would be worthy of her and show her that her confidence was not misplaced."

Nancy Edison explained things to Thomas and didn't ask him to memorize. He was paid by his father for every book that he read. One of his first books was on science. Thomas tried the experiments in the book. He wanted to see for himself how things worked. He found he liked to experiment on his own, especially with chemicals.

Thomas bought jars of chemicals with whatever money he had. After a while he had collected two hundred of them. On each he hand-lettered the label, POISON. Of course, not all the chemicals were poison, but Thomas didn't want anyone to touch his things. At first he kept the jars in his bedroom, but then he moved them to the cellar.

Strange odors, smoke, and the occasional sound of a small explosion came from the cellar laboratory. Samuel Edison didn't like it. He wanted his son playing outside like other boys his age. But Nancy Edison thought Thomas should be left alone to discover on his own the answers to some of his many questions.

During the summer of 1858, Thomas tried working outside. He and another boy planted a large field with vegetables. They tended and harvested the crop and then loaded it onto a horse-drawn wagon. The boys sold the vegetables and made a good profit. But Thomas didn't like working in the hot sun.

It was just about the time of his farming summer that Thomas became fascinated with a new invention, the telegraph. Samuel F. B. Morse applied for a patent for the telegraph in 1837. The first telegraph line, between Baltimore and Washington, was completed in 1844, just three years before Thomas was born. And in 1858, when he was eleven, Thomas made his own telegraph set. He stretched the wire to his friend James Clancy's house, a half a mile away. Thomas and James practiced sending the dots and dashes of the Morse code back and forth for hours.

3. The More to Do, the More Done

In 1859 the Grand Trunk Railroad opened a line connecting Port Huron with Detroit, some sixty miles away. A four-car train left Port Huron at seven each morning and arrived in Detroit about four hours later. The return trip began in the late afternoon. At the time, a twelve-year-old boy was not too young to begin work, and Thomas got a regular job on the train as a "candy butcher." He sold newspapers, sandwiches, fruit, and candy to passengers.

On the afternoon ride back to Port Huron, Thomas sold Detroit newspapers. At each stop, he got off the train to sell his papers to the people at or near the station. One time, he was late in catching the train. As he ran alongside it, a conductor reached out to help. He grabbed onto Thomas's ears. Thomas said that as he was being pulled aboard, he heard something in his ears crack.

Thomas began to lose his hearing about then. He felt the conductor who had tried to help him caused his deafness. But it's more likely that his deafness was caused by the scarlet fever he had as a child or the many ear infections he had which were not properly treated.

Some days, during the six-hour wait in Detroit, Thomas read in the public library. And some days he remained on the train and experimented with the jars of chemicals he kept on a shelf in the baggage car. One day a jar fell and started a fire. Thomas and a conductor put it out, but after that Thomas had to do all his experimenting at home.

The Civil War broke out in 1861, and people throughout the United States were eager for news about it. One day, in April 1862, Thomas went to the offices of the *Detroit Free Press* to pick up the newspapers he would sell on the afternoon ride back to Port Huron. There he read the news about a battle of Shiloh, near Pittsburgh Landing, Tennessee. Twenty-five thousand were already either wounded or killed and the battle was still being fought.

Thomas was certain that if people on the train and along the rail line knew about the battle, they would be anxious for a newspaper. He bought one thousand newspapers that day, instead of his usual one hundred. Then he paid the telegraph operator in Detroit to send news of the battle to all the stops along the rail line. When the train arrived at each of the stations, people crowded around Thomas. They were eager to buy copies of the newspaper. Thomas raised the price of the papers, first to a dime each, then to fifteen cents and finally, when he reached Port Huron, to twenty-five cents. He sold all one thousand newspapers and made a very good profit.

That same year, at the age of fifteen, Thomas began his own weekly newspaper. He bought an old printing press and some type. He put them in the train's baggage car and began printing the *Grand Trunk Herald*. It was filled with news of people who traveled and worked on the train. In one issue of the newspaper, Thomas wrote about his attitude toward work. ''The more to do, the more done.''

One morning, during the summer of 1862, Thomas was waiting at the Mount Clemens, Michigan station and noticed a small boy playing on the tracks. A boxcar was rolling toward him. Thomas dropped his things and ran to the boy. He quickly picked him up and carried him away.

The boy's father was James Mackenzie, the stationmaster at Mount Clemens. He rewarded Thomas for saving his son by teaching him telegraphy. Soon after that, in 1863, sixteen-year-old Thomas got his first job as a telegraph operator. He would work at telegraphy for almost six years.

4.   Telegraph Operator

IN THE SUMMER OF 1863, Thomas Edison was hired as a part-time telegraph operator in Port Huron. The office was not busy. Thomas had plenty of time for his experiments. One day at the telegraph office, while he was showing two of his friends how he mixed various chemicals, the mixture exploded. There was flying glass, a ruined telegraph, and a few slight injuries. Thomas lost his job.

In the 1860s, there was a great need for telegraph operators throughout the United States and Canada. Thomas was hired as the night telegraph operator in Stratford, Ontario, across the Canadian border. Very few messages came through at night so to ensure that he was on the job, Thomas had to send a Morse code signal—the number six—every half hour. But Thomas wanted either to rest or to be able to experiment without having to stop every half hour. He used a small clock and rigged the telegraph so the signal would be sent automatically. But he was caught and told to stay awake or find another job.

Thomas stopped using the device but later lost his job anyway. He forgot to signal "Danger" to an approaching freight train and two trains nearly collided. No one was hurt, but Thomas was called to the railroad's main office in Toronto. The general manager threatened to put Thomas in jail for his mistake. Thomas didn't wait to find out what would happen. He ran off, got on a train, and quickly left Canada.

During the next five years, Thomas traveled from city to city as he went from one job to the next. He wandered to Fort Wayne, Toledo, Indianapolis, Memphis, Louisville, New Orleans, and Cincinnati.

Thomas was a good telegrapher. He was able to send messages quickly, and he wrote the messages he received in a clear, neat handwriting. But he would rather play a practical joke or experiment with chemicals or electricity than sit by a telegraph key.

In one dangerous joke Thomas hooked a battery to a railroad yard washbasin. When the workers put their hands in the water, they got an electric shock. Thomas and a friend had a great time watching the surprised trainmen.

Thomas experimented with a ''duplex,'' a telegraph machine that could send two messages at one time over the same wire. And he invented a machine that recorded the dots and dashes of a fast incoming message more slowly so that the message could be written down neatly.

In 1868, Thomas arrived in Boston for another job as a telegrapher. Boston was an exciting city for Thomas. All around him people were busy tinkering and experimenting, including Alexander Graham Bell, who in 1876 would invent the telephone.

In 1868, Thomas began work on an automatic vote recorder. With it, a member of Congress could record his vote by simply pressing a button. A few people in Boston liked Thomas Edison's work and invested in it. And in January 1869, Thomas left his job and became a full-time inventor.

5. First Inventions

DURING HIS LIFETIME, Thomas Edison would be granted more than one thousand patents for his inventions. In June 1869, he was granted his very first patent for the vote recorder, but when he brought his invention to a committee of the Congress, it was rejected. He was told that members of the Congress did not want to press buttons. They wanted to announce their votes and try to convince others to vote the same way.

Thomas learned a lesson. He resolved never again to invent something that no one wanted.

Thomas got busy again on his duplex telegraph machine. He traveled to Rochester, New York to demonstrate it, but it didn't work. Thomas was discouraged. He decided to leave Boston and move to New York City where he hoped his luck at inventing would improve.

Thomas had almost no money. His friend, Franklin Pope, was employed by S. S. Laws's Gold Indicator Company, and he let Thomas sleep there. The company had a stock ticker that sent the changing price of gold to brokers. One day the ticker suddenly stopped. No one knew what had gone wrong. Thomas studied the machine and very soon had it going again. The owner of the company was delighted and hired Thomas.

Thomas kept the stock ticker going. He tinkered with it and improved it until the company was bought by Western Union a few months later. Thomas decided not to stay on. In October 1869, he, his friend Franklin Pope, and another partner formed Pope, Edison and Company. They would make fire and burglar alarms and electrical devices for use with telegraphy.

Thomas often said, "There is no substitute for hard work." At Pope, Edison and Company Thomas was busy from early each morning until very late at night. Within a short while he invented a telegraph which printed the price of gold and silver. The partners sold the invention to Western Union for fifteen thousand dollars. Thomas received five thousand dollars as his share, more money than he had ever made before. He wrote to his parents and offered to send them whatever money they needed.

"I never did anything worth doing by accident," Thomas once said, "nor did any of my inventions come by accident. They came by work."

Thomas continued to work hard and to invent. After a while he realized that the success of Pope, Edison and Company relied mostly on him and his inventions. He decided to work on his own.

Shortly after Thomas went into business for himself, he invented an improved stock ticker. Western Union paid him forty thousand dollars for it. Thomas took the check to the bank and came out with the money in ten- and twenty-dollar bills, more than a thousand of them, stuffed in his pockets. The next day, with the help of a friend, Thomas opened a bank account. Later he used the money to set up a shop in Newark, New Jersey, to produce the improved stock tickers for Western Union.

In Newark, Thomas met Mary Stilwell. She had long wavy hair and was then just sixteen years old. Thomas began to court her. Many years later he said that he used his deafness as an excuse to sit close to her. He told her he had to sit close to hear what she said.

Thomas and Mary married on December 25, 1871. They had three children, a daughter they named Marion Estelle and two sons, Thomas Alva, Jr., and William Leslie. Thomas nicknamed his first two children Dot and Dash after the signals used over the telegraph.

6. The Wizard of Menlo Park

THOMAS HAD A YOUNG, growing family at home, but he spent most of his time at his shop. At times he worked through the night without stopping for sleep. And when he did sleep, it was often just a short nap on a desk or workbench.

Thomas was busy inventing. By 1875 he had already received patents on more than one hundred inventions or improvements of existing machines. He invented the mimeograph machine, waxed paper, and the quadruplex, which enabled four telegraph messages to be sent over one wire at the same time.

Christopher Sholes had invented the first typewriter and received a patent for it in 1868, but the letters wandered out of line. Thomas Edison helped him make a typewriter which Thomas later said, "gave fair results."

Then, late in 1875, Thomas felt he needed a better place to work. His mother Nancy had died four years earlier. Thomas wrote to his father and asked him to come to New Jersey and look for a place for him to build a laboratory.

Samuel Edison found Menlo Park, a small New Jersey town with several farms and a few houses. There he supervised the building of a long two-story building. All around the outside of the laboratory was a picket fence to keep out pigs, cows, and other animals which otherwise might wander in. Inside there were tables, benches, science books, various kinds of instruments, and jars filled with chemicals.

The telephone had just been invented by Alexander Graham Bell. The original Bell telephone received sound well, but the sound it sent was weak. Thomas Edison experimented with improving it. Of course, because of his poor hearing, it was difficult for him to hear the sounds, so he had others listen for him.

Thomas discovered that by using tiny pieces of carbon he could send a loud, clear sound. He sold his carbon transmitter to Western Union. They eventually sold it to the Bell Telephone Company, which combined the carbon transmitter with the Bell receiver.

Thomas's experiments with the telephone led him to work on the phonograph, a machine that could save sounds and replay them later. First Thomas used waxed paper, then tinfoil. He wrapped the tinfoil around a cylinder. As he spoke, a diaphragm attached to a needle vibrated and made grooves in the tinfoil.

When the device was ready, Thomas gathered his workers. He turned the cylinder. The needle made grooves in it as he recited, ''Mary had a little lamb.'' Then he changed the needle and the diaphragm to one which would replay the sounds. He turned the cylinder again and, as he said later, ''I was never so taken aback in my life.'' The workers could clearly hear the nursery rhyme.

Thomas demonstrated the phonograph before the United States Congress and then to the president of the United States, Rutherford B. Hayes. Thomas was called ''The Wizard of Menlo Park.''

But Thomas knew that his success was not the result of wizardry. It took hard work. "Genius," he said, "is one percent inspiration and ninety-nine percent perspiration."

The phonograph was not ready for public use. The sounds it made were still very weak. But Thomas was ready to move on. He was interested in experimenting with electricity. He hoped to produce a usable electric light.

During the 1870s gaslights were used to light homes and city streets. But smoke from the burning gas damaged walls and curtains. There was danger of fire, and if some of the gas didn't burn, there was danger from the poisonous fumes. Electric arc lights were already being used. But these were much too bright for use in the home.

Thomas Edison first studied how artificial light was produced. His notes filled hundreds of books. Then he experimented. He said at the time, "I speak without exaggeration when I say that I have considered three thousand theories in connection with electric light."

He experimented for more than a year with different filaments, wires that could burn and glow without melting when electricity passed through them. He finally settled on cotton thread rolled in carbon and then baked. To keep the filament from burning out too quickly, he needed to keep it away from oxygen. He pumped the air out of a glass bulb and placed the filament inside.

There were many other devices needed to make the light useful, including switches, sockets, lamps, fuses, and insulation for the electric wires. Thomas Edison had more than a hundred people working on them.

Stories of the new lights were printed in newspapers and magazines. People came to Menlo Park to see them. And once people saw the lights, they wanted them for their homes. Thomas Edison set up various companies to produce the light bulbs and lamps needed for this new form of light.

In 1881, at the French Electrical Exposition in Paris, Thomas displayed his work. He brought everything there—a huge dynamo to generate electricity, the wires, the lamps, and the lights. Thomas won five gold medals in Paris and was made an officer in the French Legion of Honor. Soon after that he set up companies to bring electric light to France, Italy, Holland, Belgium, and England.

In 1882 in New York City, Thomas set up the Pearl Street Station to generate electricity. In September electricity was used to provide light for the first eighty-five customers. The light was described as "soft, mellow and grateful to the eye." To those working by the light, it seemed almost like working by daylight.

Thomas Alva Edison was a celebrity. People came from great distances to see his lights and to see him. Sarah Bernhardt, the most famous actress of the time, called Thomas a "creative genius." In the coming years Thomas would meet other famous people, including William "Buffalo Bill" Cody, Louis Pasteur, Henry Ford, J. P. Morgan, and President Herbert Hoover. And those people were all proud to say they met Thomas Alva Edison, the inventor of the incandescent lamp, what today we call the electric light bulb.

7. Short on Time

THOMAS EDISON was famous, but in many ways he hadn't changed. He was still curious, still mischievous. He still enjoyed a practical joke.

Thomas also enjoyed smoking cigars. He kept a box in his desk, but they seemed to disappear faster than he was smoking them. It was time, he felt, to teach the cigar thief a lesson. He bought a box of trick cigars filled with paper and hair and put them in his desk. But this time the joke was on Thomas. He was so busy with his work that he forgot all about the trick cigars. He smoked them all himself.

Thomas continued to work hard, at times almost without stopping for several days. He often did not see his family for weeks. Then, in July 1884, he was shaken when illness struck his wife Mary. She was stricken with typhoid fever. Thomas stayed with her. Then, on August 9, 1884, at the age of just twenty-nine, Mary Stilwell Edison died.

Thomas still had his work. It still took much of his time. But without a wife, without Mary, he was lonely.

There were undoubtedly a great number of unmarried women interested in meeting "The Wizard of Menlo Park." Through his friends Thomas was introduced to many of them.

In 1885, he met Mina Miller, a bright woman half his age. Thomas was immediately attracted to her. He thought about her constantly. At one time he taught her Morse code. Some time later he tapped a question to her: "Will you marry me?" She tapped back "Yes." On February 24, 1886, Thomas Alva Edison and Mina Miller were married. They had three children together, Madeline, Charles, and Theodore.

Thomas and Mina moved into a large house in West Orange, New Jersey. Nearby he built a laboratory many times bigger than the one in Menlo Park. In it he stored everything he might need for his experiments and inventions, including thousands of jars of chemicals and every size screw, needle, and wire he could find, as well as all sorts of other materials.

Thomas and the more than fifty people working for him improved some of his old inventions and worked on some of his new ideas, too. Thomas developed a more useful phonograph with better sound. Then, in 1887, he placed a tiny phonograph inside a small tin doll. With the turn of a crank the doll seemed to talk. Thousands of the dolls were sold.

Not all of Thomas Edison's ventures were successful, however. He bought nineteen thousand acres of New Jersey land which he planned to mine for iron ore. He lost more than one million dollars on this, but he said he had a "good time spending it." Thomas also went into the cement business. He did better at that.

Thomas Edison developed a kinetoscope, a box which showed moving pictures, and a fluoroscope which was a great help to medical surgery. Thomas worked for many years on an electric car. It ran well, but it never had the success of the gasoline-powered cars. The storage battery he developed for the car, however, found many uses.

In December 1914, fire destroyed his laboratory. Thomas Edison was sixty-seven years old, but he was not ready to stop work. His best friend, Henry Ford, lent him money to rebuild, and Thomas Edison continued his work.

During the First World War, Thomas worked on devices to save American ships from German torpedoes. He worked on camouflage so American troops could be hidden from attack. At the time, Thomas was proud to say, ''I never invented weapons to kill.''

Early in 1931, Thomas Edison said, "I am long on ideas but short on time. I expect to live to be only about a hundred." But Thomas Edison didn't live that long. He died on October 18, 1931, at the age of eighty-four.

Thomas Edison was issued 1,093 patents, more than any other inventor. He was an inventive genius, a genius who worked very hard. The things he worked on, the light bulb, the system to bring electricity into our homes, the phonograph, and motion pictures changed our world.

INDEX

In loving memory of my inventive
and heroic brother, EDWARD M. ADLER,
recipient of The Carnegie Hero's Award,
1948-1979 —D.A.A.

Text copyright © 1990 by David A. Adler
Illustrations copyright © 1990 by Lyle Miller
Printed in the United States of America

Library of Congress Cataloging-in-Publication Data
Adler, David A.
Thomas A. Edison, great inventor : a first biography /
written by David A. Adler; illustrated by Lyle Miller. — 1st ed.
p.   cm.
Summary: A biography of the inventive genius who
developed the electric light bulb,
the phonograph, and the motion picture.
ISBN 0-8234-0820-5
1. Edison, Thomas A. (Thomas Alva), 1847-1931 —
Juvenile literature.   2. Inventors—United States—
Biography—Juvenile literature.
[1. Edison, Thomas A. (Thomas Alva), 1847-1931.
2. Inventors.]   I. Miller, Lyle, 1950-   ill.   II. Title
TK140.E3A63   1990
621.3092—dc20   [B]   [92]   89-77507   CIP   AC